For information regarding permission, write to:
Disney Licensed Publishing, 114 Fifth Avenue, New York, New York 10011
ISBN 0-7172-6746-6

Printed in the U.S.A.
First printing, January 2003

DISNEY'S
Lady and the Tramp II
· SCAMP'S ADVENTURE ·

SCHOLASTIC INC.

New York   Toronto   London   Auckland   Sydney
Mexico City   New Delhi   Hong Kong   Buenos Aires

Lady and Tramp thought they were very lucky dogs.
They lived with a loving family—Jim Dear, his wife
Darling, and their young son Junior.

And Lady and Tramp had a lively family of their own. The girls—Annette, Colette, and Danielle—were just like Lady. Their son's name was Scamp, and he looked just like his father.

But Scamp didn't always think he was such a lucky dog. He thought he had to follow too many rules!

No matter how hard Scamp
tried, he always seemed to break the rules.
"Scamp!" Tramp would scold, "you know you're
not supposed to climb on the furniture."

And it seemed Scamp was always having baths.
"When you live in a house, you need to be clean,"
Tramp would patiently remind his son.

Scamp couldn't even play with Junior without getting into trouble. They both loved to play tug-of-war. But even that usually ended in a scolding for Scamp as soon as Jim Dear saw his hat.

"Scamp!" Jim Dear shouted. "I've told you a thousand times . . . NO!" Then Jim Dear would sigh and hang up his chewed hat with the others.

One day, things got
out of hand. Junior
threw a ball out of
the window, and Scamp
jumped out to get it.

Scamp raced
back inside, trailing
mud all through the
house. It was too
much for Jim Dear.
"This time, you've
gone too far!" Jim
shouted.

Then the
worst happened.
Jim Dear took
Scamp outside and chained him up!
   Even Jim felt awful. "I'm sorry, pal,
but I just don't know what else to do."

Scamp was miserable.

Tramp tried to comfort his son. "Now, Scamp, sometimes it's hard being part of a family. You have to obey certain rules."

"But I want to run wild and free like a real dog!" the young pup cried.

"Son, the world out there is full of traps," his father explained. "Here, you have a family who loves you."

But Scamp didn't feel as if he belonged, and he still wished he could run free.

After Tramp left, a little dog about Scamp's age peeked through the fence. Her name was Angel, and Scamp thought she was the sweetest dog he had ever seen.

She looked at Scamp and smiled. Then she disappeared behind the fence with some other dogs.

Poor Scamp. He wanted to go and play with her. He pulled and pulled at the chain and finally he broke free!

"Wait for me!" Scamp shouted after her. But she had gone. Scamp wandered the streets, searching for Angel. The sky grew dark. But Scamp didn't care. He was on an adventure—free from rules and baths!

Then Scamp heard some dogs howling. He followed the sound and came upon some dogs in a junkyard. Scamp couldn't believe it. The dogs were running and jumping all over the place.

Just then Scamp spotted Angel standing in a corner.

As he walked into the junkyard, Scamp noticed two dogs playing tug-of-war with a hat. He saw another lounging on a sofa. This was the life Scamp wanted! He was sure he had finally found the place where he belonged!

All of a sudden the leader of the pack, Buster, noticed the pup. "Nobody joins the Junkyard Dogs unless I say so. What's your name, Sport?" Buster asked.

"Name's Scamp," the pup answered.

Buster wasn't sure if Scamp had what it took to become a Junkyard Dog. As the sun rose, Buster decided he'd have to test Scamp.

Back at home, Lady went out to the yard with Scamp's breakfast. When she saw the broken chain, she knew Scamp had run away. Lady raced inside to get help.

When Jim Dear and Darling found out that Scamp was gone, they were very upset.

"Did you call the pound?" Jim Dear asked.

"Yes, dear. They haven't seen him," Darling answered.

Worried sick, Jim Dear decided to search for Scamp with Lady and Tramp.

They didn't know Buster had taken Scamp to a
narrow alley in the city. "You gotta pass a little test
of courage . . . in Reggie's alley," Buster announced.

Then Buster threw a can into the darkness. "Fetch
the can outta the alley," Buster challenged.

All the Junkyard Dogs watched in horror as Scamp slowly walked into the alley. Scamp followed a rumbling sound and almost bumped into a huge dog sleeping in the shadows. Scamp realized this must be Reggie.

Scamp almost got away—but he made a noise that woke up Reggie. The large dog growled and began to chase Scamp!

Scamp tore out of the alley. As he turned a corner, he found Angel caught in the dogcatcher's net. Thinking fast, Scamp managed to free Angel . . . and get Reggie trapped. All the Junkyard Dogs were impressed with Scamp.

The pack of dogs wandered over to the park.

"Hey! You . . . saved my life," Angel said to Scamp. "Nobody else here would've dared to do that."

Scamp said proudly, "I'm gonna be the best Junkyard Dog there ever was!"

Then the Junkyard Dogs told him about a dog called Tramp—the greatest street dog ever.

Just hearing Tramp's name made Buster angry. "He met this girl, see. Queen of the kennel-club set . . . Lady. He left the streets for the cushy pillow life," Buster recalled.

Scamp couldn't believe what he'd heard. His own father had been a street dog.

Buster stared at Scamp who was scratching behind his ear. "Hey! The Tramp used to scratch like that. You ain't related, are ya?" Buster asked.

"No way," Scamp said, too afraid to tell Buster the truth.

Scamp
left the park
with Angel.
As the two
talked, Angel
told Scamp that
she had lived with
families before. "Just
when I'd start to think,
'Wow, this is my family,'
they'd move, or have a new baby.
And I'm out on the street."

But Angel wanted to be in a family again. She
couldn't understand why Scamp liked the streets.
She was sure his family missed him.

And they did. Jim Dear, Lady, and Tramp kept on
searching. But by that evening, they still
hadn't found any trace of Scamp.

Scamp and Angel wandered the streets together.
They came across an Italian restaurant. When the
owner saw the two hungry pups, he served them a
big plate of spaghetti and meatballs.

Scamp was falling in love
with Angel. Of course, that didn't
mean that Scamp was going to
share the last meatball!

Afterwards, Scamp and Angel walked by Scamp's house. A minute later, Jim Dear, Lady, and Tramp returned home. "Oh, no! We gotta get out of here!" Scamp said, pushing Angel behind a bush.

Tramp and Lady stayed
outside to talk. Attempting to
cheer up Tramp, Lady said,
"Oh, we'll find him. You were
the best street dog there ever
was, and I still have faith in
the old Tramp."

Angel was stunned when
she heard Tramp's name.
"The Tramp is your father?"
she asked. Angel couldn't
believe Scamp would run away
from such a loving family.

Scamp tried to explain that
he needed to be wild and free,
as the two of them ran off.

The next day, Scamp and Angel joined the other
Junkyard Dogs in the park. They saw Jim Dear,
Darling, Junior, Aunt Sarah, and her Siamese cats Si
and Am having a picnic. But Jim Dear and Darling
were too worried about Scamp to enjoy the picnic.

Aunt Sarah tried to calm them down. "Scamp
will be all right," she said.

When Buster overheard Scamp's name mentioned and saw his enemy Tramp, he knew that Scamp was Tramp's son. Buster was furious and ordered Scamp to take another test. If Scamp really wanted to be a Junkyard Dog, he would steal his family's chicken.

Scamp agreed to do it!

Scamp raced down the hill and snatched the chicken. Terrified, Si and Am jumped onto Aunt Sarah, causing her to toss the potato salad into the air. It landed on top of Jim Dear's head.

Tramp was furious and took off after his son.

Tramp quickly caught up with Scamp.

"I'm NOT going home," Scamp announced. "It's great out here on the streets. But then, you know all about that, don't you?" Scamp added.

Tramp apologized for not telling Scamp that he had been a street dog. "I didn't want that life for you. Because I found something better. I found love," Tramp explained.

Tramp was asking Scamp to return home when Buster turned up. Buster convinced the young dog to stay on the streets.

Although it was difficult, Tramp knew Scamp would have to learn his lesson the hard way.

"When you've had enough, our door is always open," Tramp said to Scamp as he walked away.

Buster took off Scamp's collar to show he was no longer a family dog.

Scamp was thrilled. "Woo-hoo! I'm a Junkyard Dog!" he yelled, and all the Junkyard Dogs crowded around to congratulate him.

Tramp returned
to the picnic. "He
wouldn't come home,"
he sadly told Lady.
"But Tramp! He belongs at home,
with us!" Lady insisted.
"I'm afraid we're just going to
have to let him figure this one out
on his own. He'll come to his
senses," Tramp hoped.

Buster led the other dogs back to the junkyard.

"How could you do that? He's your father, go after him!" Angel scolded. "You're good. And decent. Kind. The streets will beat that out of you if you stay," she warned.

Angel begged Scamp to leave the junkyard with her to find a nice family where they could both stay. Scamp refused and Angel left the junkyard alone.

It wasn't long before Scamp missed Angel. Sad
and lonely, Scamp searched the empty streets, talking
to himself. "I didn't mean it, Angel," Scamp said.
"I don't know what I was thinking."

Angel overheard him as he walked past.

Suddenly the dogcatcher
turned a corner and
spotted Scamp.

Scamp took off like a rocket.
But the dogcatcher nabbed him.

"Well, lookee here.
No collar. It's a one-way
trip to the pound for
you," the dogcatcher
said, laughing.

On the way to the pound, the truck passed Angel.

"Scamp!" Angel yelled, racing after them. But she couldn't keep up. So she rushed to Scamp's home. "Hurry! Scamp's in trouble," she yelled to Lady and Tramp.

Tramp raced after Angel.

Meanwhile, Scamp was definitely in danger. He was locked in a cage with Reggie!

But just as Reggie was about to attack, Tramp stormed into the pound. "Hold on, Scamp!" he shouted as he knocked the cage latch open.

Tramp quickly outwitted Reggie. Soon father and son walked out of the pound together.

Scamp realized that the streets were too dangerous.
He wanted to be with his family and Angel.

So Scamp headed back to the junkyard to get his
collar back from Buster. "I'm going home . . . where
I belong," he announced.

Along the way, Scamp admitted to his father, "I
shouldn't have run away." Then Scamp turned to
Angel and said, "Thanks for saving me from the
pound, Angel."

When they heard barking, the entire family
rushed outside.

Junior giggled. "Scamp! I love you!" he cried.

Jim Dear patted Scamp on the head. "It's so
good to have you back where you belong!" he said.

Scamp noticed Angel watching the happy family outside the gate, and he started barking.

"Jim Dear, I think Scamp brought a friend home," Darling said.

Jim Dear bent down, "Welcome to the family!" he said to Angel.

And it was a happy little family—baths and all!